GRAPHIC MYTHICAL CREATURES

FIREBIRDS

BY GARY JEFFREY
ILLUSTRATED BY SARA CAPPOLI

Gareth Stevens
Publishing

Please visit our website, www.garethstevens.com.
For a free color catalog of all our high-quality books,
call toll free 1-800-542-2595 or fax 1-877-542-2596.

Library of Congress Cataloging-in-Publication Data

Jeffrey, Gary.
Firebirds / Gary Jeffrey.
p. cm. — (Graphic mythical creatures)
Includes index.
ISBN 978-1-4339-6757-3 (pbk.)
ISBN 978-1-4339-6758-0 (6-pack)
ISBN 978-1-4339-6755-9 (library binding)
1. Birds—Folklore. I. Title.
GR735.F57 2012
598—dc23

2011022843

First Edition

Published in 2012 by
Gareth Stevens Publishing
111 East 14th Street, Suite 349
New York, NY 10003

Copyright © 2012 David West Books

Designed by David West Books

Photo credits:
p4b, Bernard Gagnon; p5br, Leoboudv, Magica

Printed in China

CPSIA compliance information: Batch #DW12GS: For further information contact Gareth Stevens, New York, New York at 1-800-542-2595.

CONTENTS

A Blaze of Glory

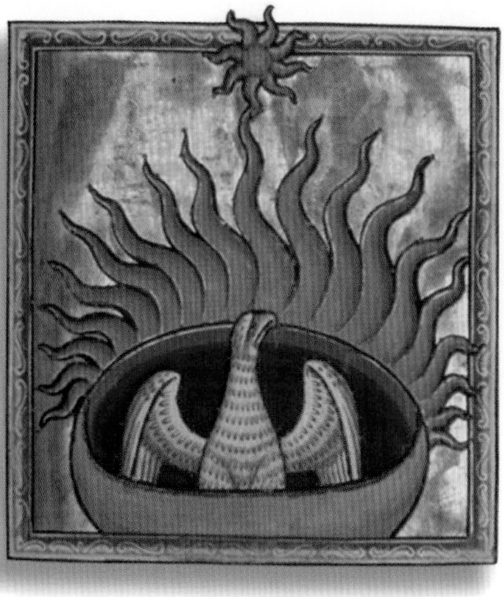

A firebird rises in a 12th-century illuminated manuscript from England.

The firebird is a mythical creature that can be found in cultures around the world. Born of fire and immortal, the firebird is either a spectacular prize or a flaming beacon of hope.

The Phoenix

The ancient Egyptians told of a red-colored bird that carried an egg to the temple of the sun in Heliopolis every 500 years. Inside the egg were the ashes of its parent. The bird would build a nest and be consumed by fire. A new bird would emerge from the burnings–the phoenix rising from the ashes.

The phoenix myth was spread by the ancient Greeks, but versions of it can also be found in the East. This golden garuda, or sun bird, (below) is on a temple in Japan.

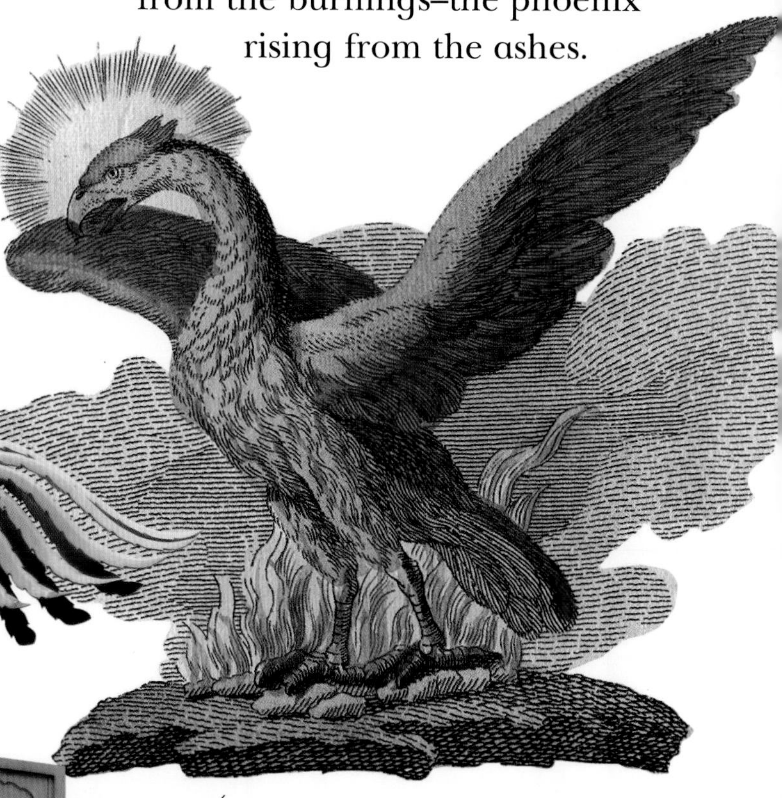

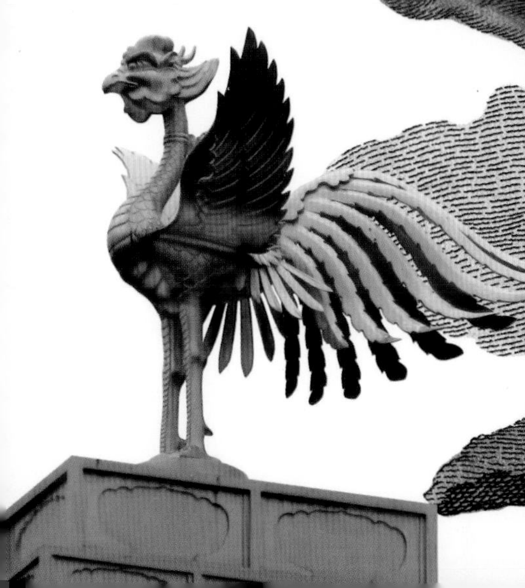

The Russian Firebird

In Russian myths, the firebird is usually a highly sought-after prize. It has jewel-like eyes and magical feathers that glow in the dark. Once captured, the firebird can bring good luck or terrible misfortune to whoever owns it.

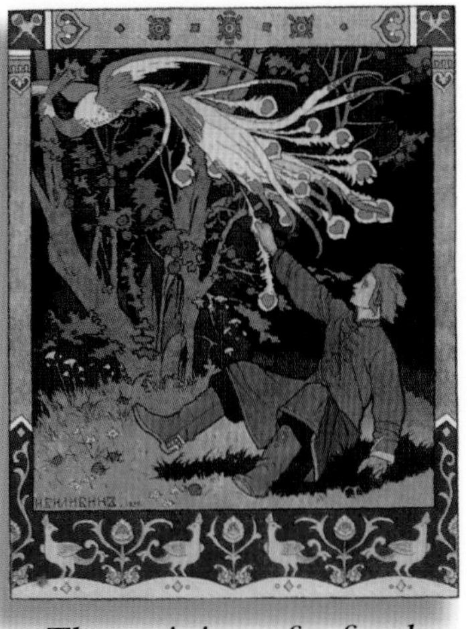

The gaining of a feather is an important part of all Russian folktales about the firebird.

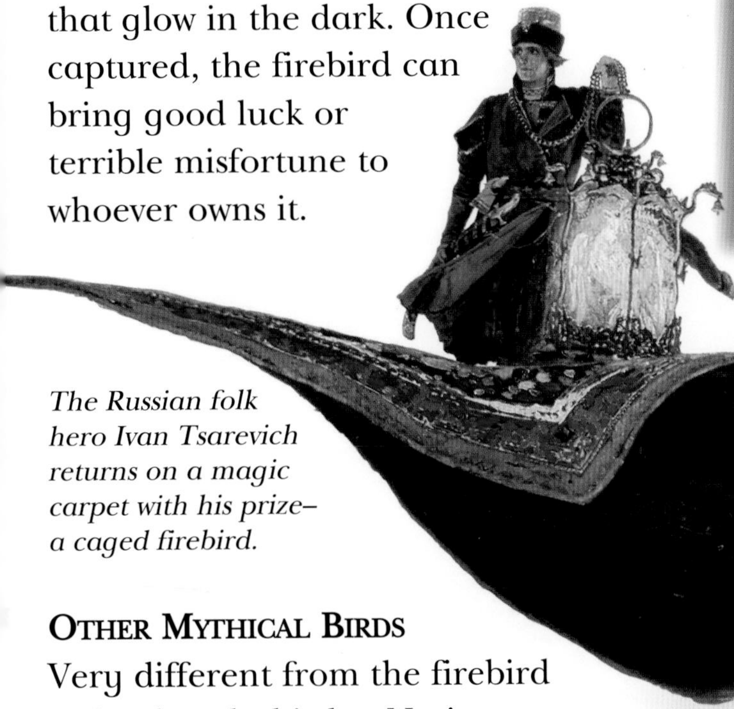

The Russian folk hero Ivan Tsarevich returns on a magic carpet with his prize–a caged firebird.

Other Mythical Birds

Very different from the firebird is the thunderbird–a Native American storm god whose wing beats make claps of thunder. Another is the Gandaberunda from India, which has two heads and can carry an elephant in the talons of each foot!

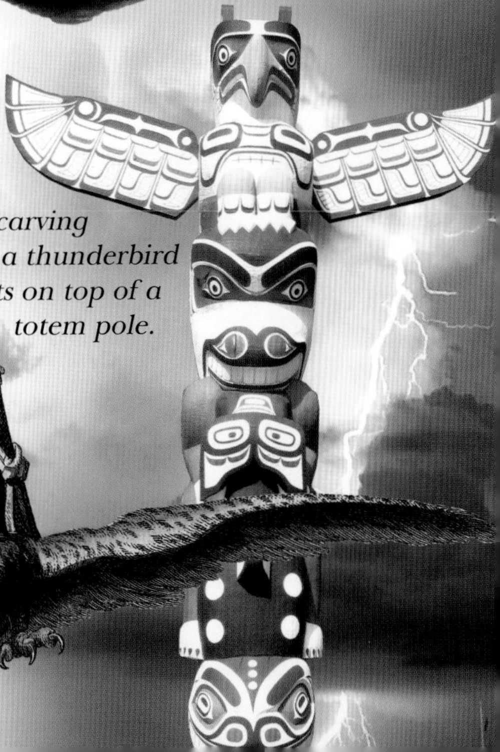

A carving of a thunderbird sits on top of a totem pole.

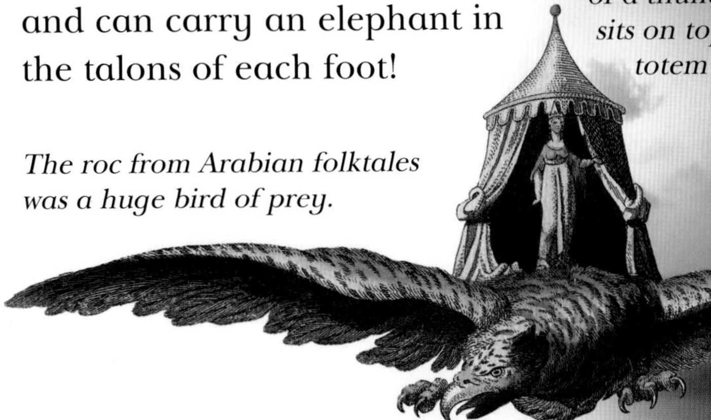

The roc from Arabian folktales was a huge bird of prey.

Prince Ivan, the Firebird, and the Wolf

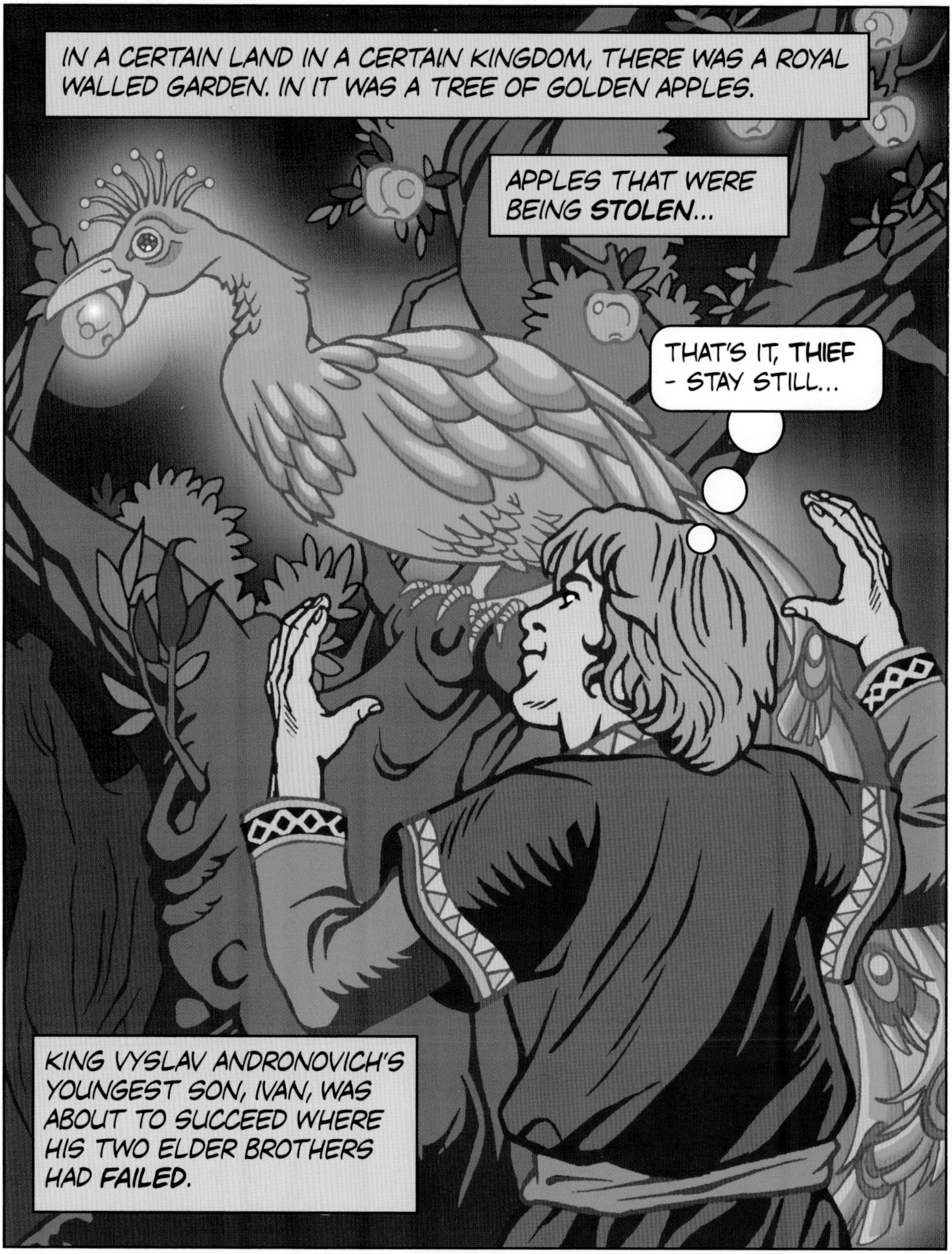

IN A CERTAIN LAND IN A CERTAIN KINGDOM, THERE WAS A ROYAL WALLED GARDEN. IN IT WAS A TREE OF GOLDEN APPLES.
APPLES THAT WERE BEING STOLEN...
THAT'S IT, THIEF - STAY STILL...
KING VYSLAV ANDRONOVICH'S YOUNGEST SON, IVAN, WAS ABOUT TO SUCCEED WHERE HIS TWO ELDER BROTHERS HAD FAILED.

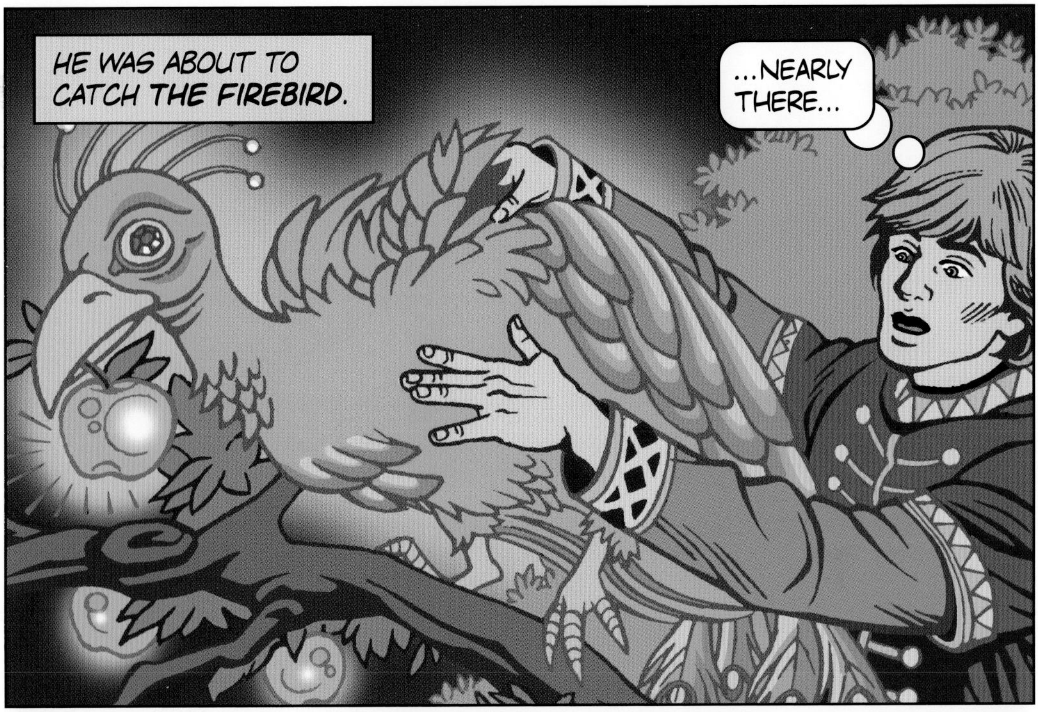
HE WAS ABOUT TO CATCH THE FIREBIRD.
...NEARLY THERE...

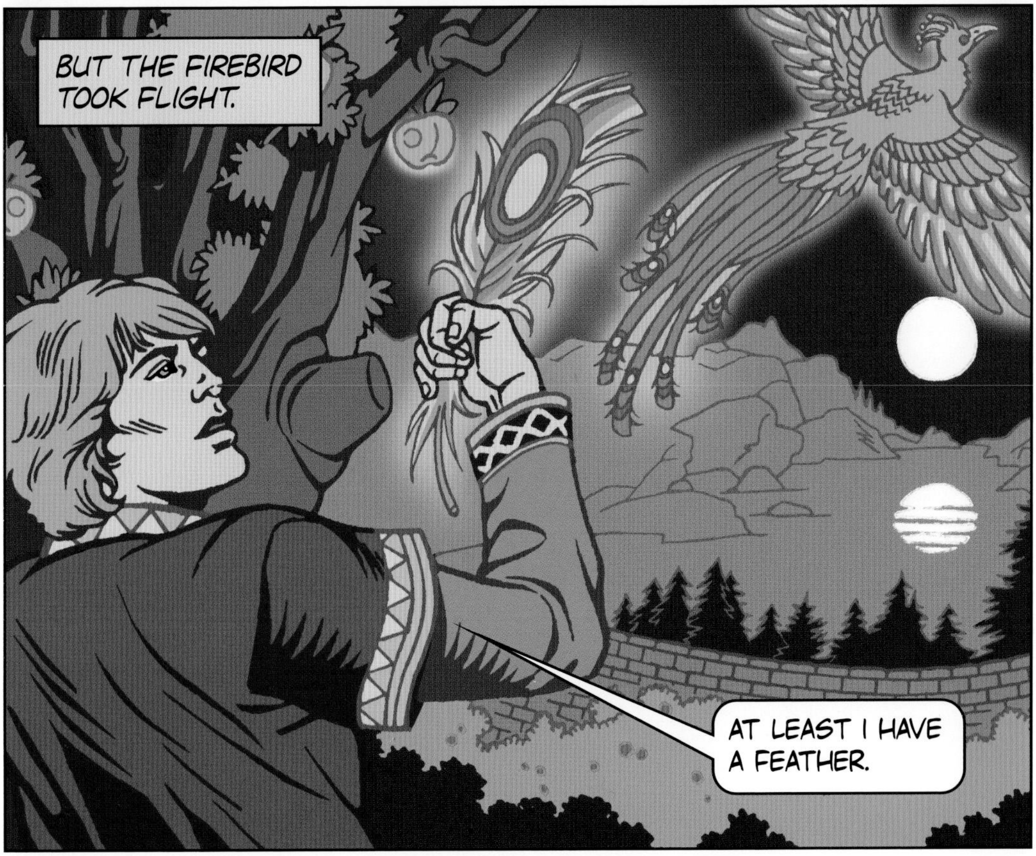
BUT THE FIREBIRD TOOK FLIGHT.
AT LEAST I HAVE A FEATHER.

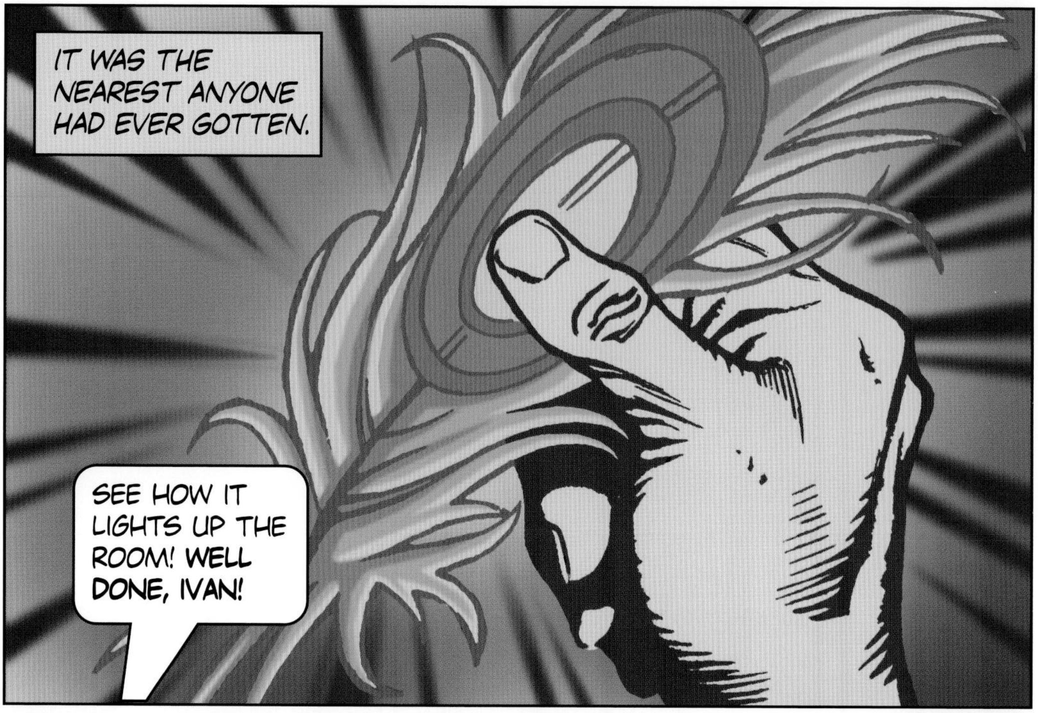
IT WAS THE NEAREST ANYONE HAD EVER GOTTEN.
SEE HOW IT LIGHTS UP THE ROOM! **WELL DONE, IVAN!**

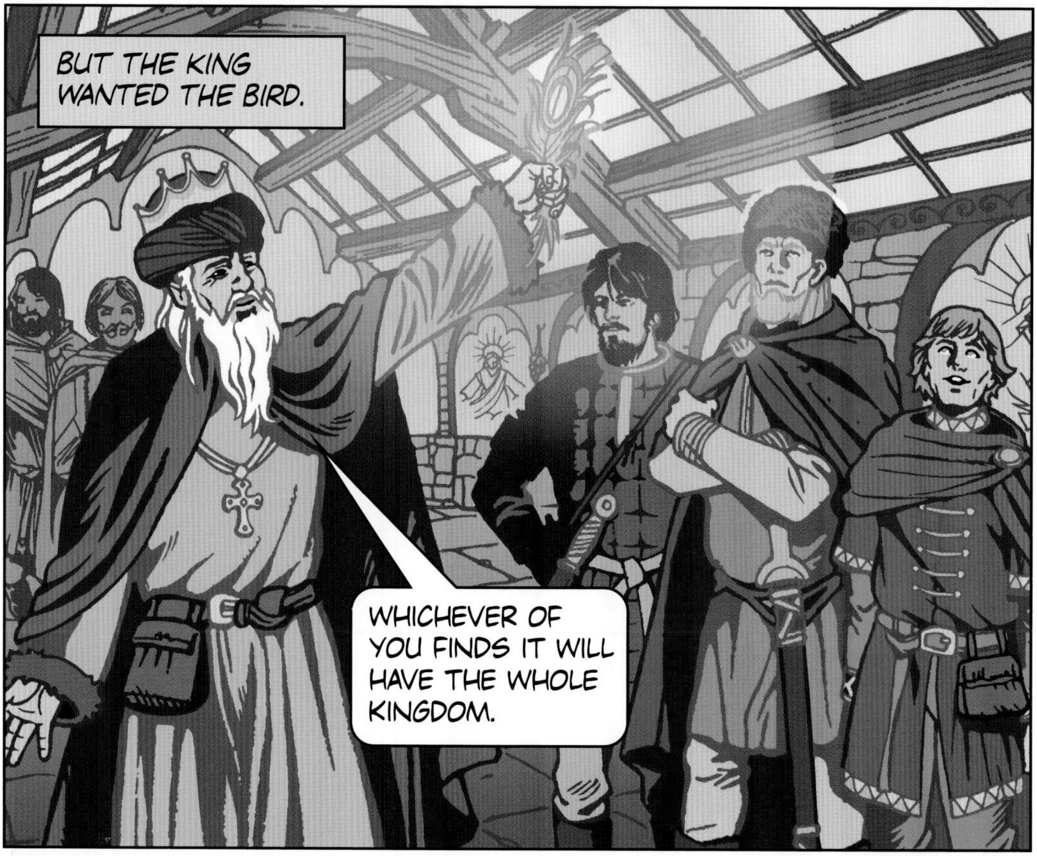
BUT THE KING WANTED THE BIRD.
WHICHEVER OF YOU FINDS IT WILL HAVE THE WHOLE KINGDOM.

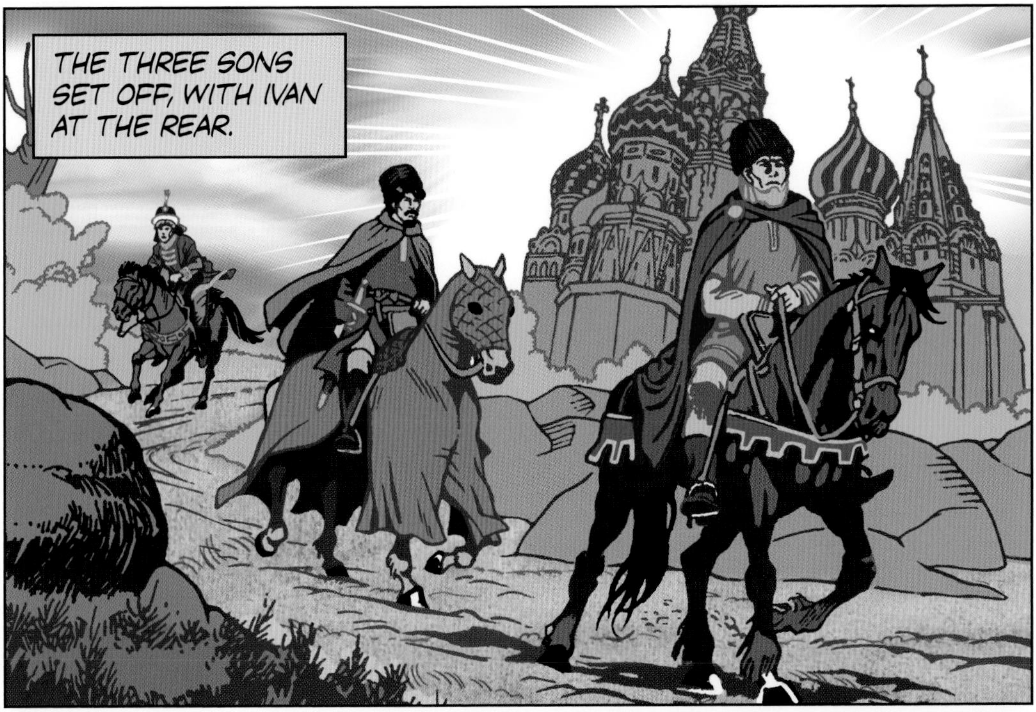
THE THREE SONS SET OFF, WITH IVAN AT THE REAR.

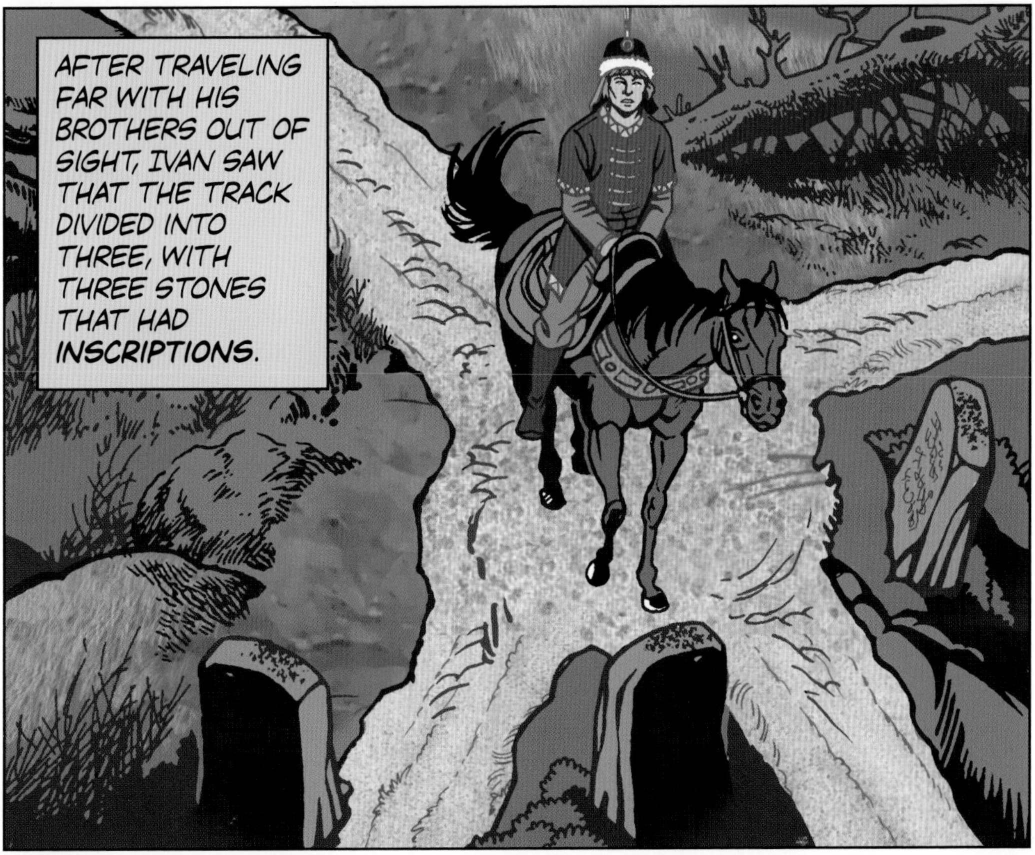
AFTER TRAVELING FAR WITH HIS BROTHERS OUT OF SIGHT, IVAN SAW THAT THE TRACK DIVIDED INTO THREE, WITH THREE STONES THAT HAD **INSCRIPTIONS**.

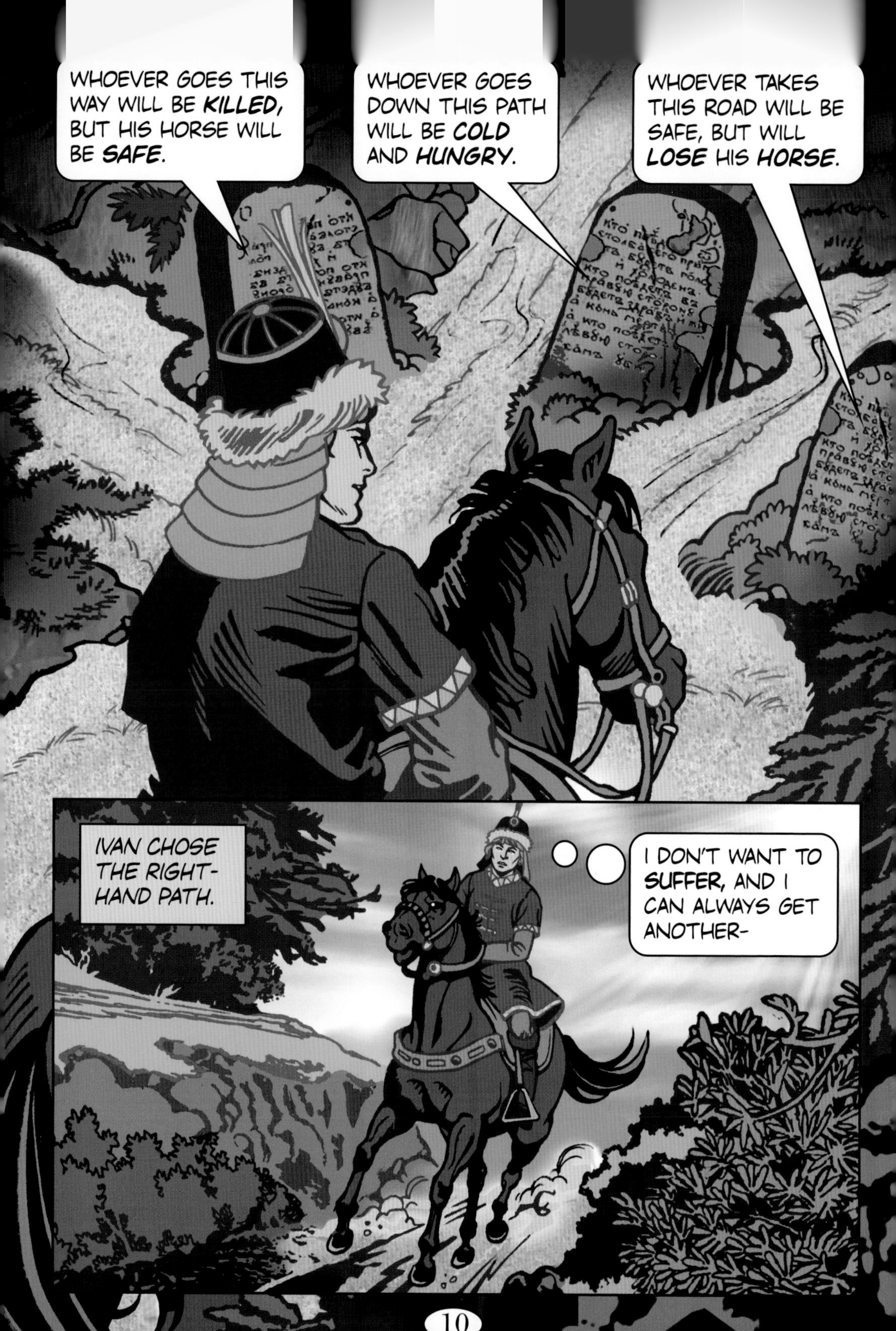
WHOEVER GOES THIS WAY WILL BE **KILLED,** BUT HIS HORSE WILL BE **SAFE**.
WHOEVER GOES DOWN THIS PATH WILL BE **COLD** AND **HUNGRY**.
WHOEVER TAKES THIS ROAD WILL BE SAFE, BUT WILL **LOSE** HIS **HORSE**.
IVAN CHOSE THE RIGHT-HAND PATH.
I DON'T WANT TO **SUFFER,** AND I CAN ALWAYS GET ANOTHER-

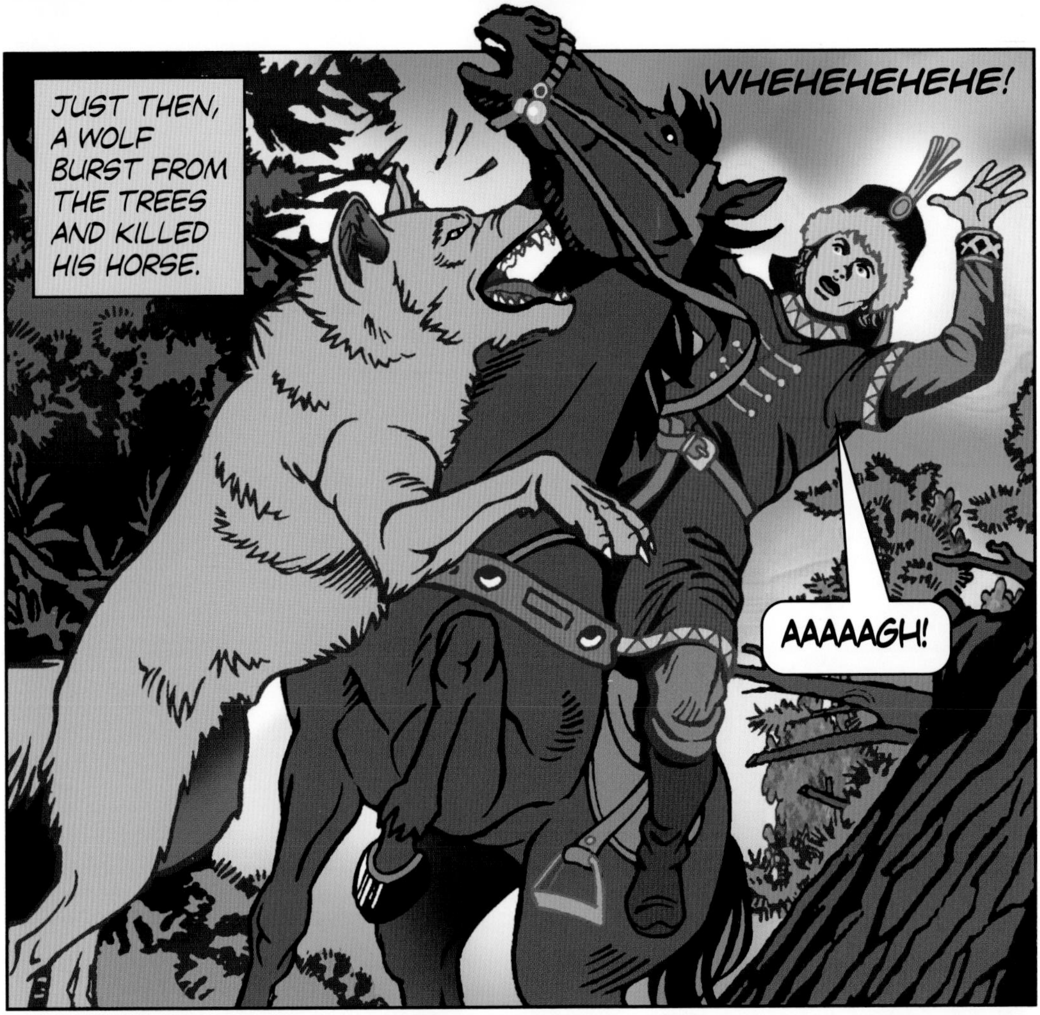
JUST THEN, A WOLF BURST FROM THE TREES AND KILLED HIS HORSE.
WHEHEHEHEHEHE!
AAAAAGH!

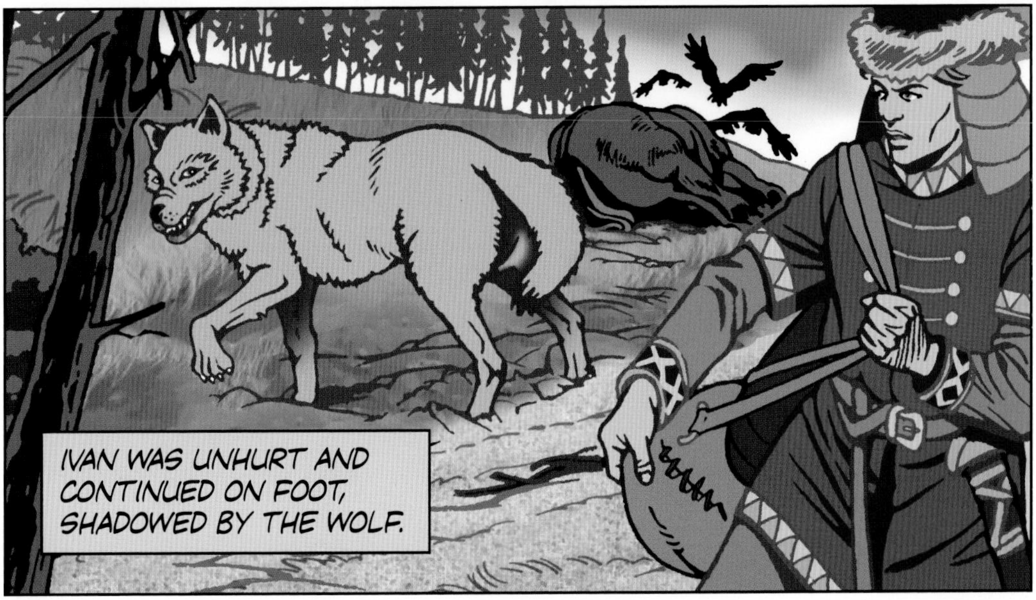
IVAN WAS UNHURT AND CONTINUED ON FOOT, SHADOWED BY THE WOLF.

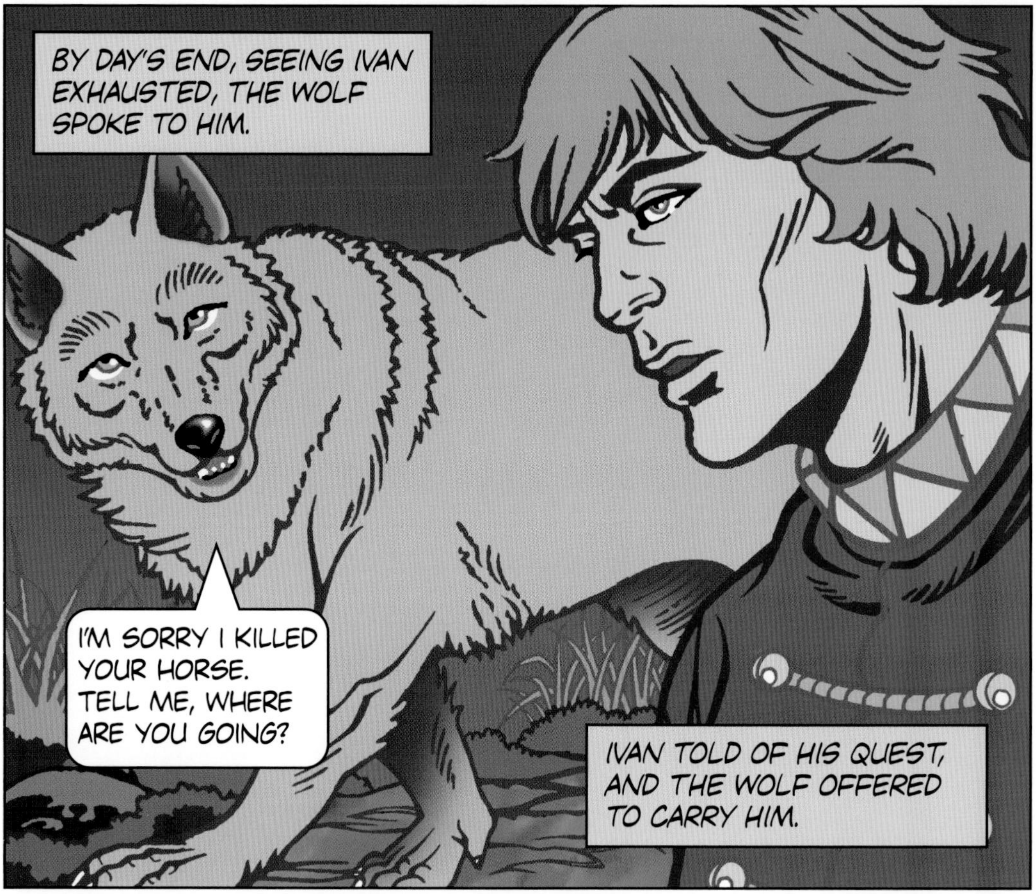
BY DAY'S END, SEEING IVAN EXHAUSTED, THE WOLF SPOKE TO HIM.
I'M SORRY I KILLED YOUR HORSE. TELL ME, WHERE ARE YOU GOING?
IVAN TOLD OF HIS QUEST, AND THE WOLF OFFERED TO CARRY HIM.

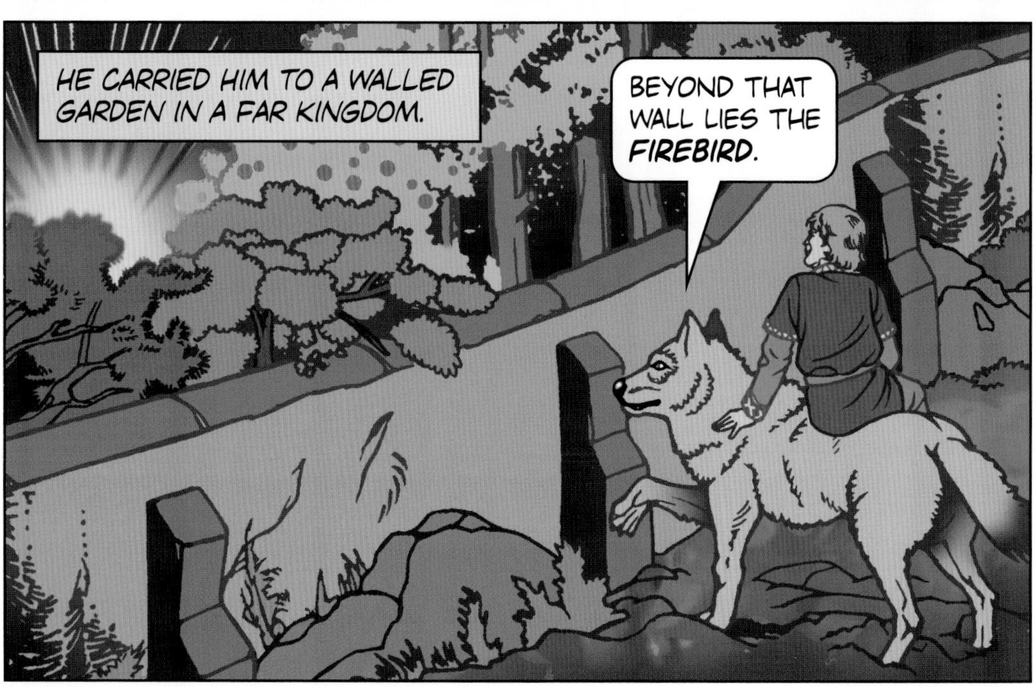
HE CARRIED HIM TO A WALLED GARDEN IN A FAR KINGDOM.
BEYOND THAT WALL LIES THE **FIREBIRD**.

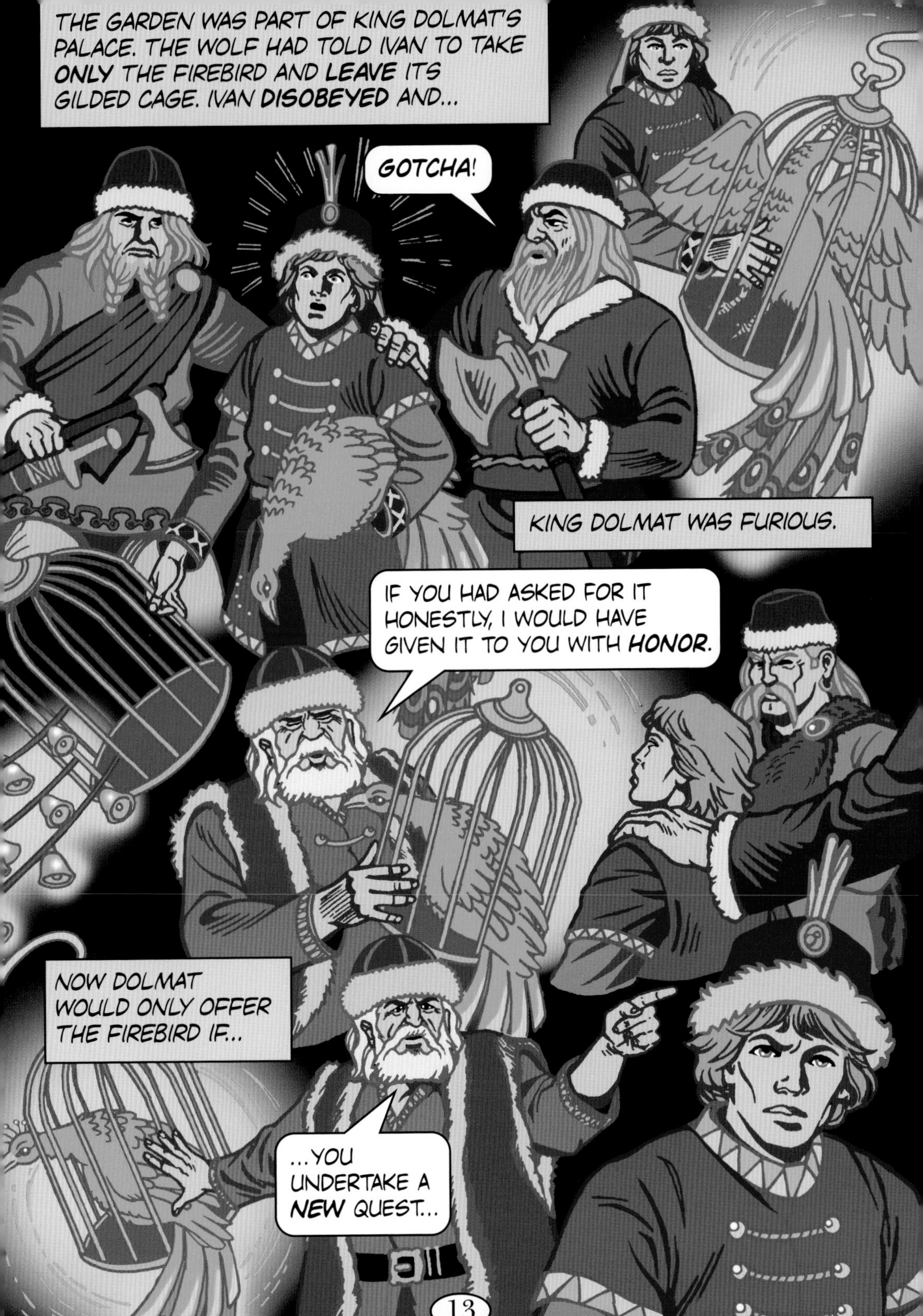
THE GARDEN WAS PART OF KING DOLMAT'S PALACE. THE WOLF HAD TOLD IVAN TO TAKE **ONLY** THE FIREBIRD AND **LEAVE** ITS GILDED CAGE. IVAN **DISOBEYED** AND...
GOTCHA!
KING DOLMAT WAS FURIOUS.
IF YOU HAD ASKED FOR IT HONESTLY, I WOULD HAVE GIVEN IT TO YOU WITH **HONOR**.
NOW DOLMAT WOULD ONLY OFFER THE FIREBIRD IF...
...YOU UNDERTAKE A **NEW** QUEST...

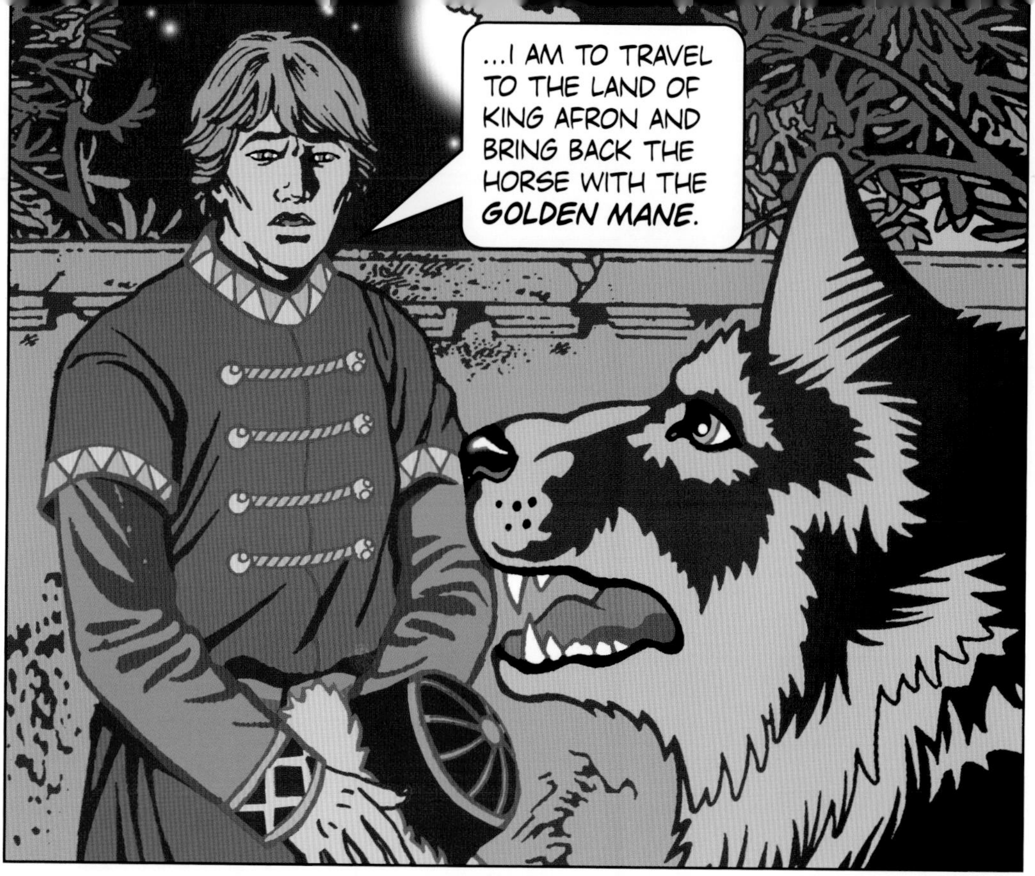
...I AM TO TRAVEL TO THE LAND OF KING AFRON AND BRING BACK THE HORSE WITH THE GOLDEN MANE.

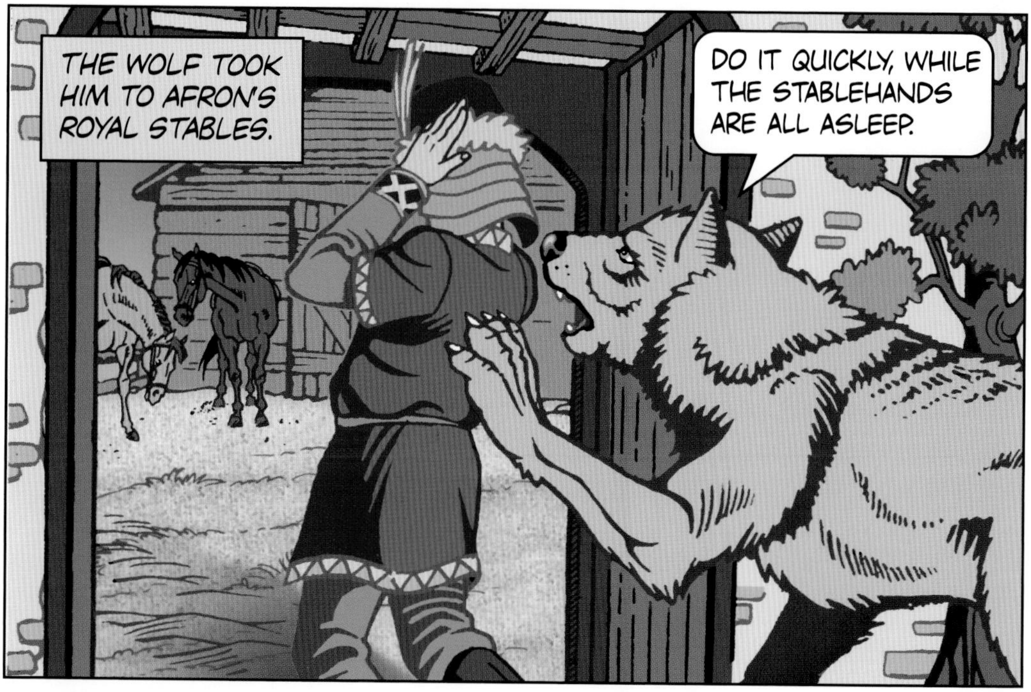
THE WOLF TOOK HIM TO AFRON'S ROYAL STABLES.
DO IT QUICKLY, WHILE THE STABLEHANDS ARE ALL ASLEEP.

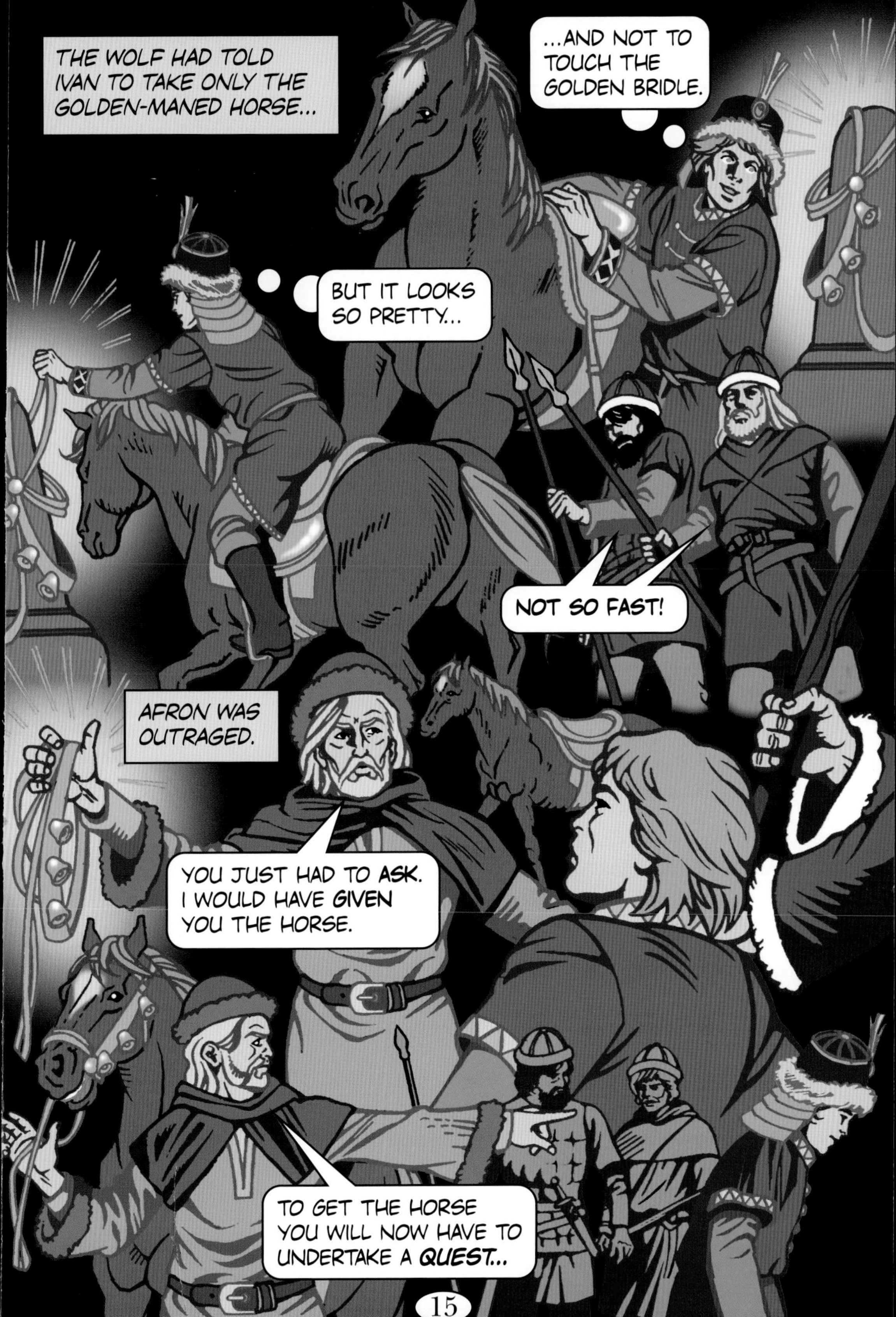
THE WOLF HAD TOLD IVAN TO TAKE ONLY THE GOLDEN-MANED HORSE...
...AND NOT TO TOUCH THE GOLDEN BRIDLE.
BUT IT LOOKS SO PRETTY...
NOT SO FAST!
AFRON WAS OUTRAGED.
YOU JUST HAD TO **ASK**. I WOULD HAVE **GIVEN** YOU THE HORSE.
TO GET THE HORSE YOU WILL NOW HAVE TO UNDERTAKE A ***QUEST***...

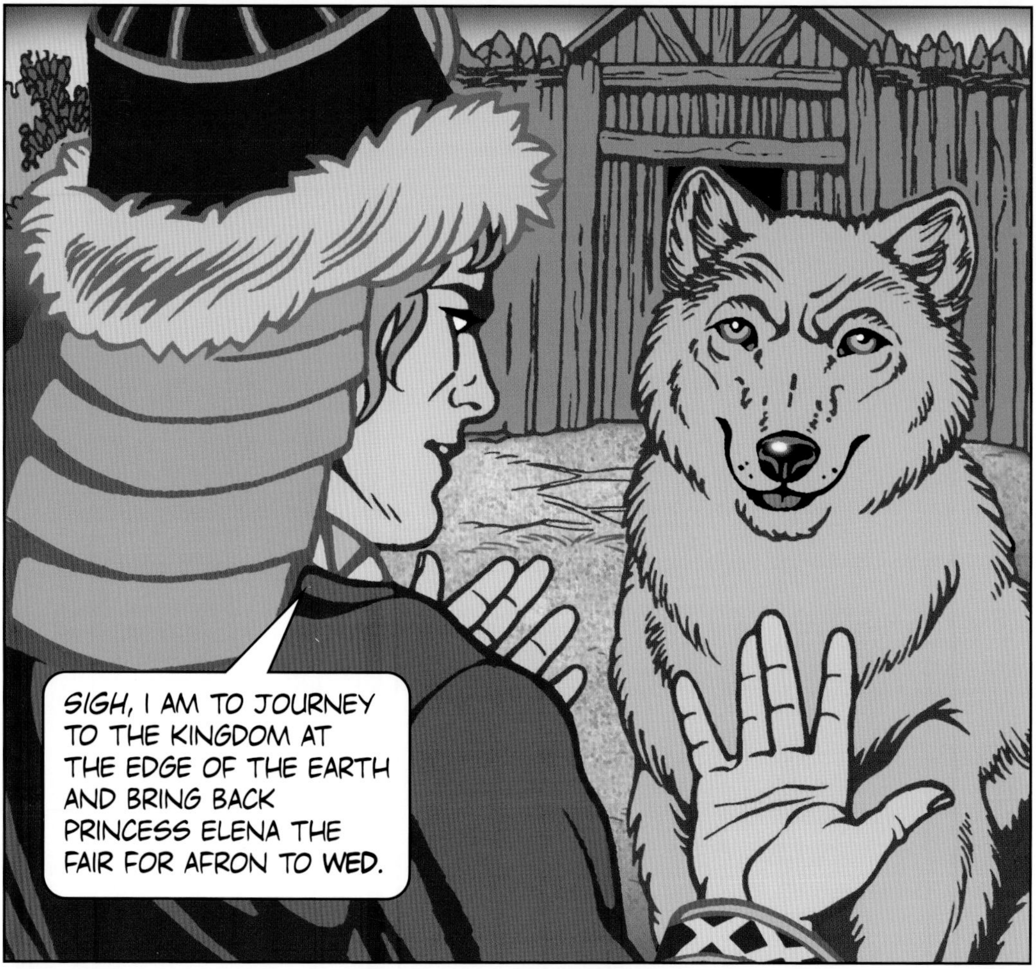
SIGH, I AM TO JOURNEY TO THE KINGDOM AT THE EDGE OF THE EARTH AND BRING BACK PRINCESS ELENA THE FAIR FOR AFRON TO WED.

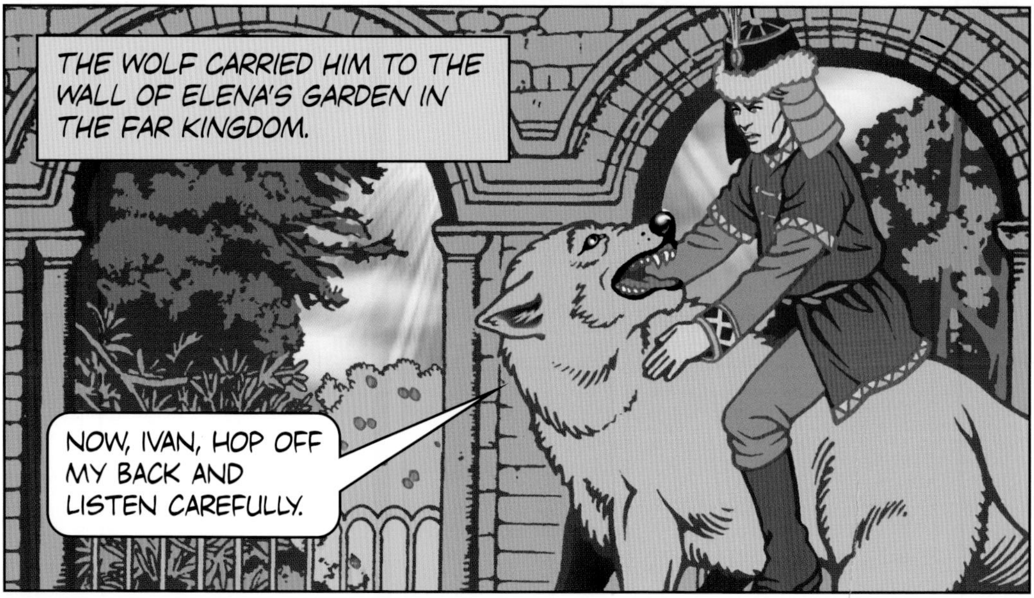
THE WOLF CARRIED HIM TO THE WALL OF ELENA'S GARDEN IN THE FAR KINGDOM.
NOW, IVAN, HOP OFF MY BACK AND LISTEN CAREFULLY.

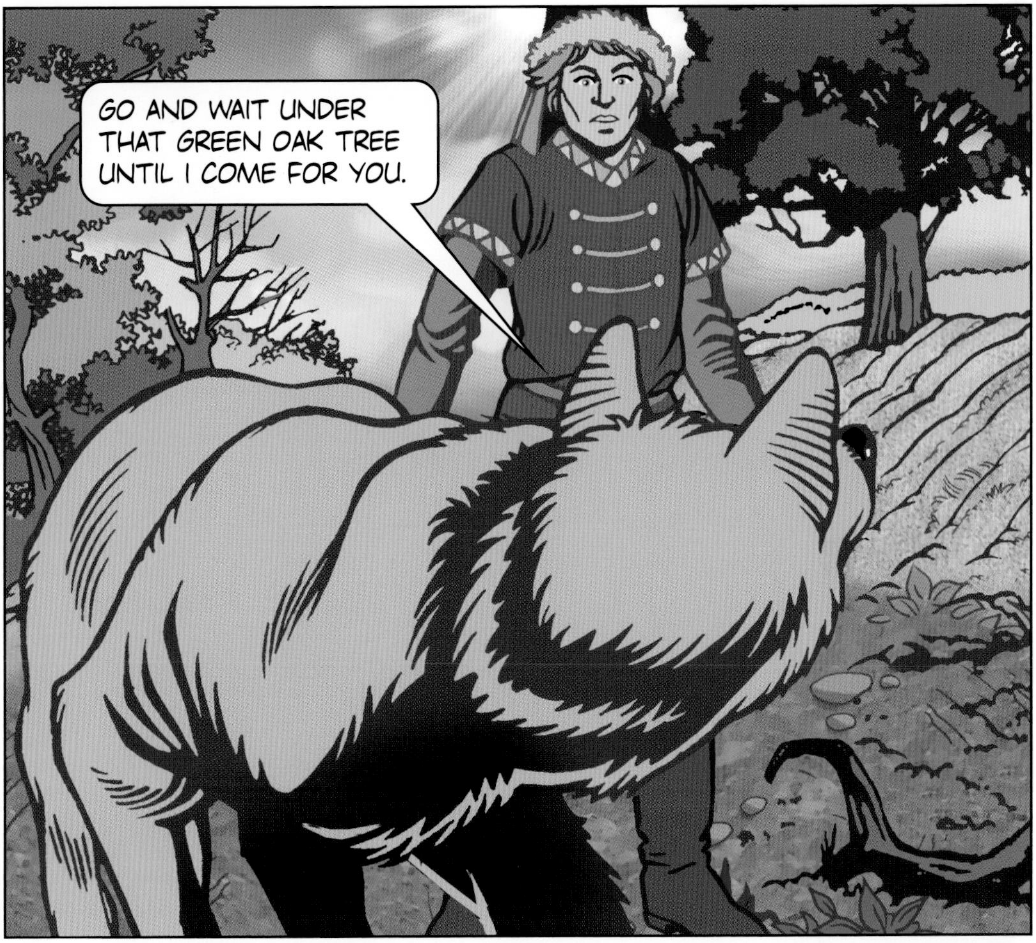
GO AND WAIT UNDER THAT GREEN OAK TREE UNTIL I COME FOR YOU.

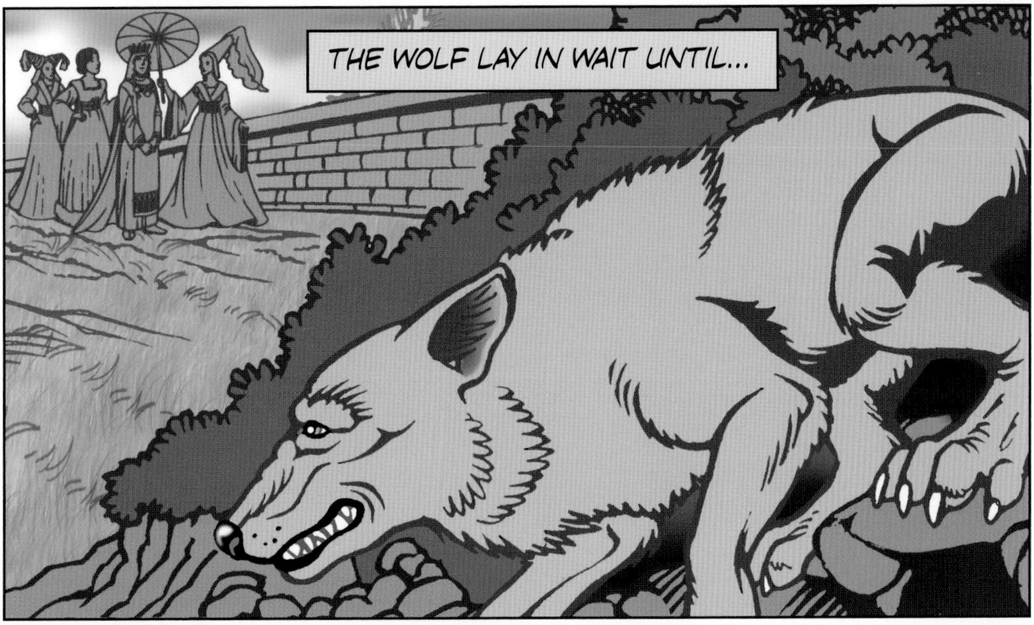
THE WOLF LAY IN WAIT UNTIL...

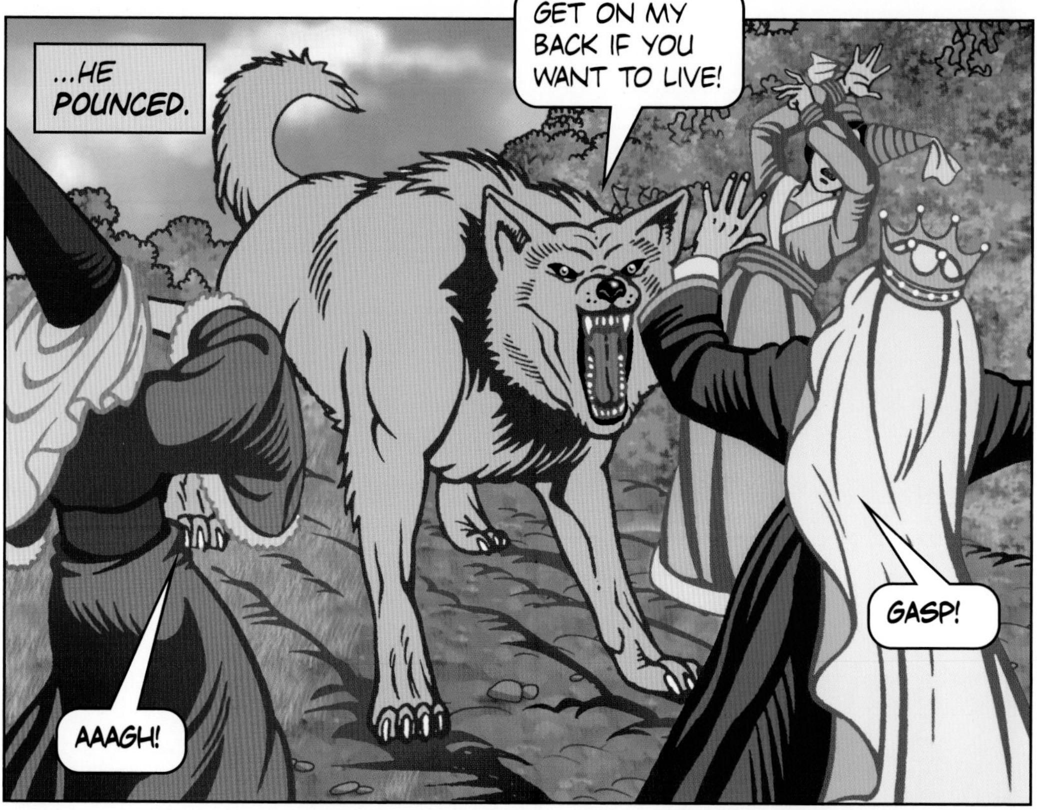
...HE POUNCED.
GET ON MY BACK IF YOU WANT TO LIVE!
GASP!
AAAGH!
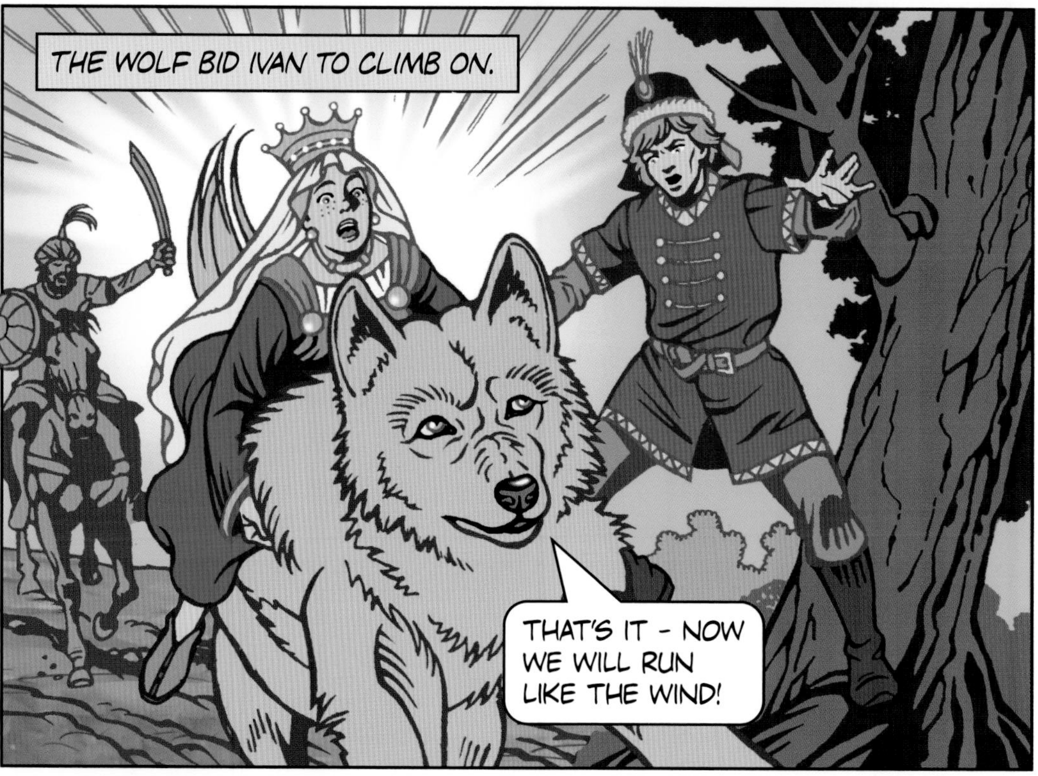
THE WOLF BID IVAN TO CLIMB ON.
THAT'S IT - NOW WE WILL RUN LIKE THE WIND!

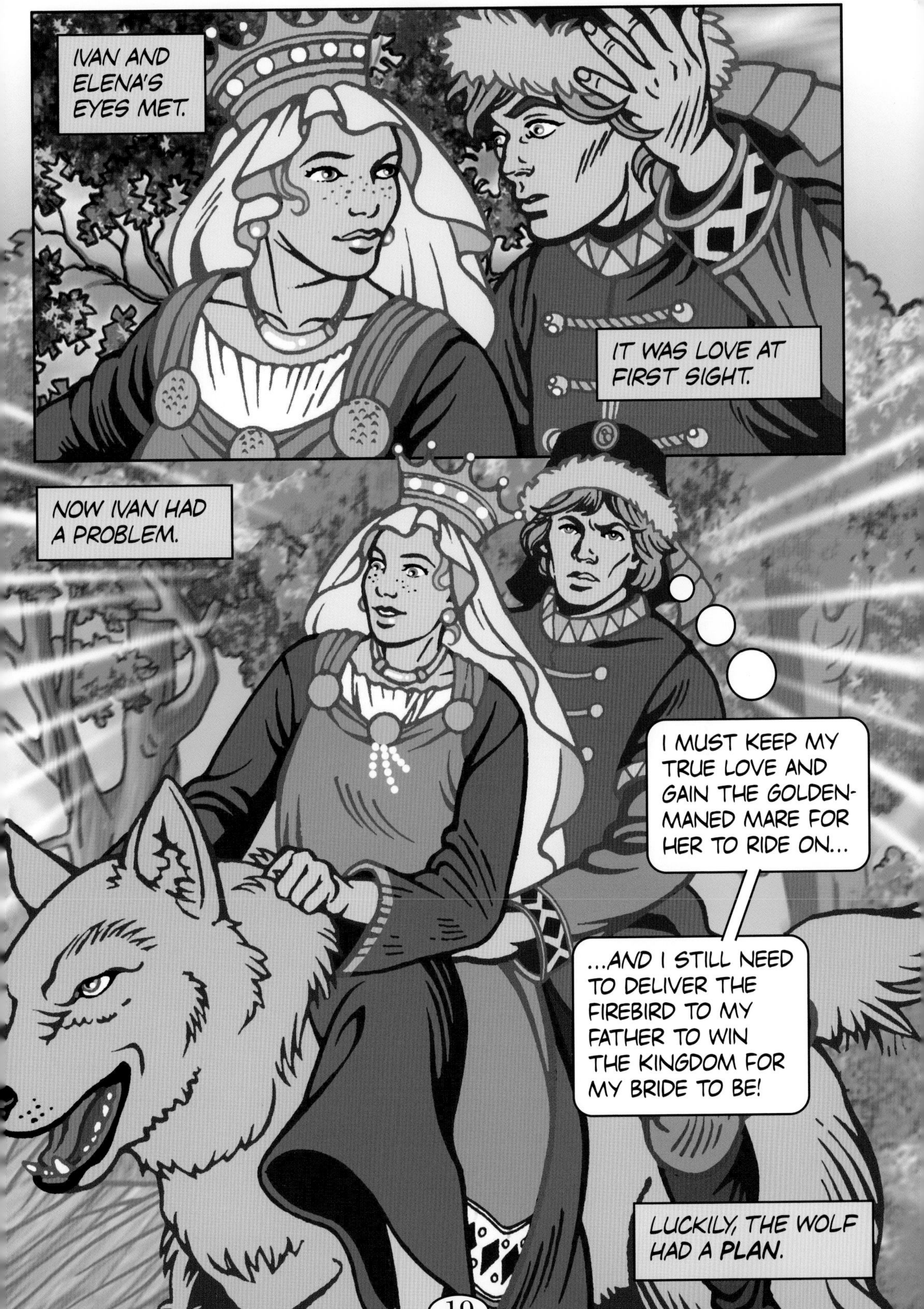

IVAN AND ELENA'S EYES MET.
IT WAS LOVE AT FIRST SIGHT.
NOW IVAN HAD A PROBLEM.
I MUST KEEP MY TRUE LOVE AND GAIN THE GOLDEN-MANED MARE FOR HER TO RIDE ON...
...AND I STILL NEED TO DELIVER THE FIREBIRD TO MY FATHER TO WIN THE KINGDOM FOR MY BRIDE TO BE!
LUCKILY, THE WOLF HAD A **PLAN**.

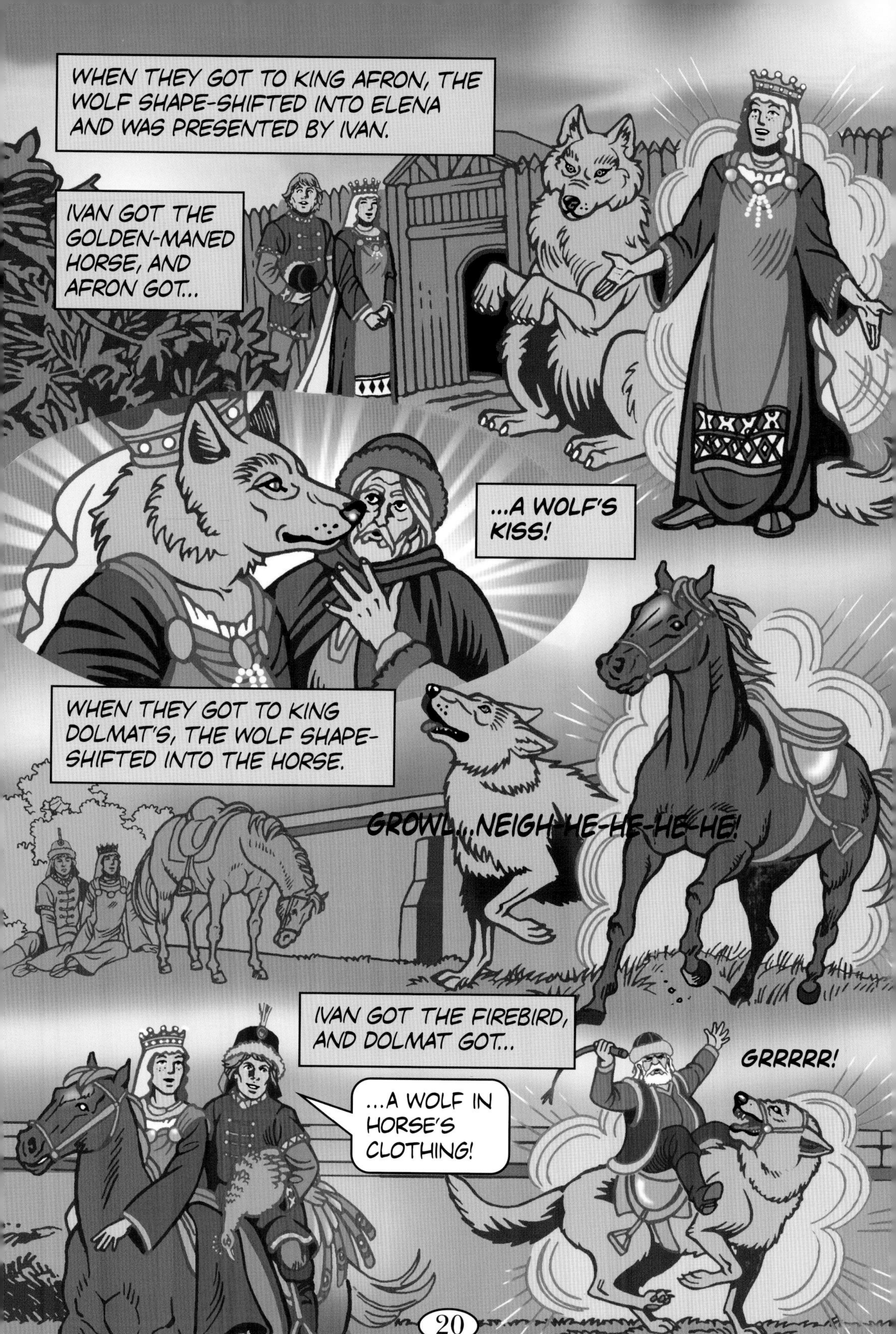
WHEN THEY GOT TO KING AFRON, THE WOLF SHAPE-SHIFTED INTO ELENA AND WAS PRESENTED BY IVAN.
IVAN GOT THE GOLDEN-MANED HORSE, AND AFRON GOT...
...A WOLF'S KISS!
WHEN THEY GOT TO KING DOLMAT'S, THE WOLF SHAPE-SHIFTED INTO THE HORSE.
GROWL...NEIGH-HE-HE-HE-HE!
IVAN GOT THE FIREBIRD, AND DOLMAT GOT...
...A WOLF IN HORSE'S CLOTHING!
GRRRRR!

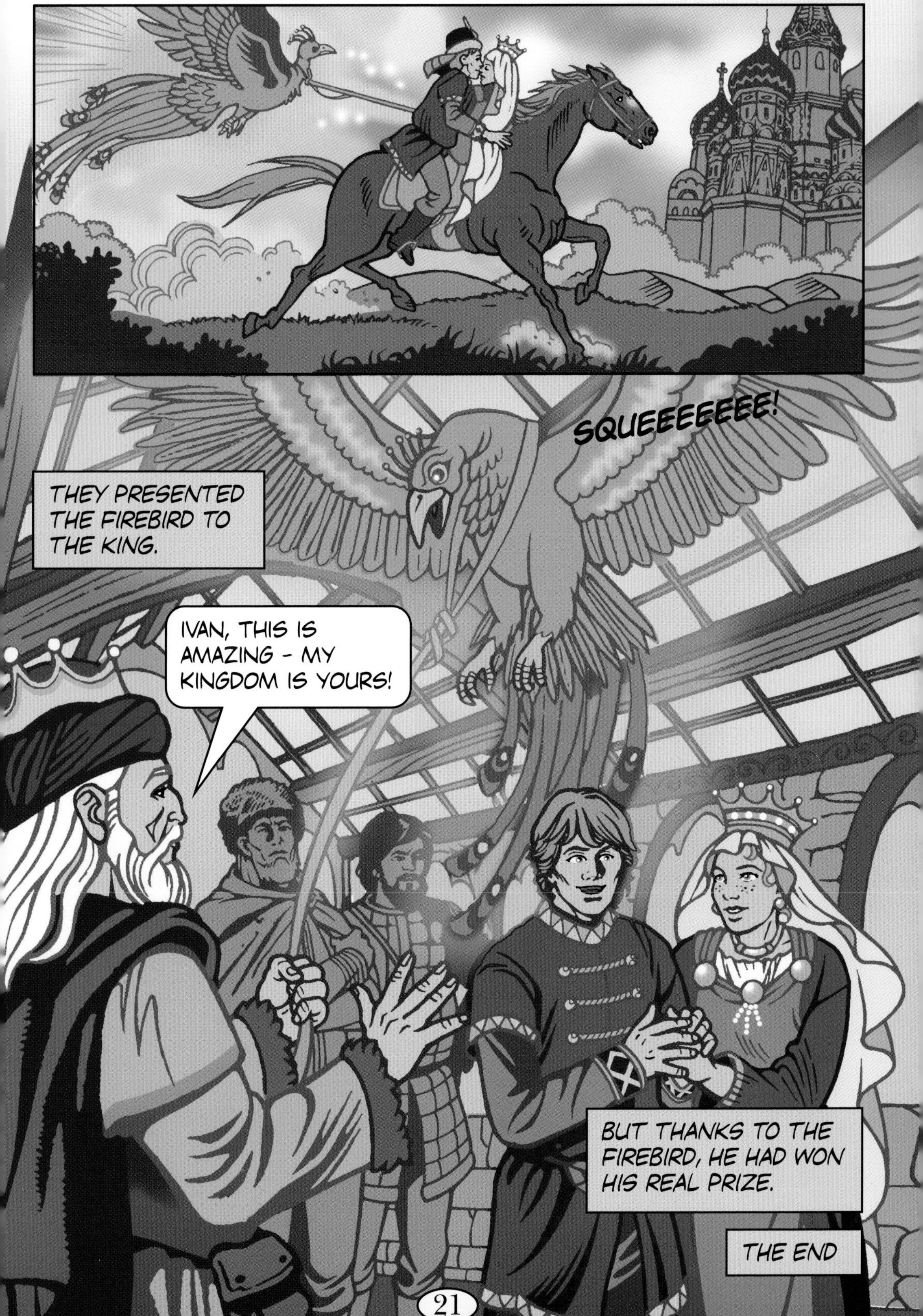
SQUEEEEEEE!
THEY PRESENTED THE FIREBIRD TO THE KING.
IVAN, THIS IS AMAZING - MY KINGDOM IS YOURS!
BUT THANKS TO THE FIREBIRD, HE HAD WON HIS REAL PRIZE.
THE END

Other Firebird Tales

Although Ivan and the Gray Wolf is the most often told firebird story, there are others…

The Firebird, the Horse of Power, and the Princess Vasilissa

A royal huntsman finds a firebird's feather. Ignoring his horse's warning, he picks it up. The king finds out and demands he bring the firebird. The huntsman and his horse catch the firebird by spreading corn across a field. Having received the firebird, the king demands that the beautiful Princess Vasilissa be brought to him. They lure the princess into a tent and kidnap her. The princess demands her wedding gown, which is at the bottom of the sea. A giant crab is battled before the huntsman defeats the king and marries the princess.

The Humpbacked Pony

Ivan the Fool gains some horses and a humpbacked pony. On the way to the fair, he finds a firebird's feather. Against the pony's advice, he keeps it. The tsar finds out about the feather and orders Ivan to get the firebird. A long quest follows involving a maiden, a lost ring, a whale(!), and a dunking in boiling and ice-cold liquids. Ivan eventually gets the girl and gains the kingdom.

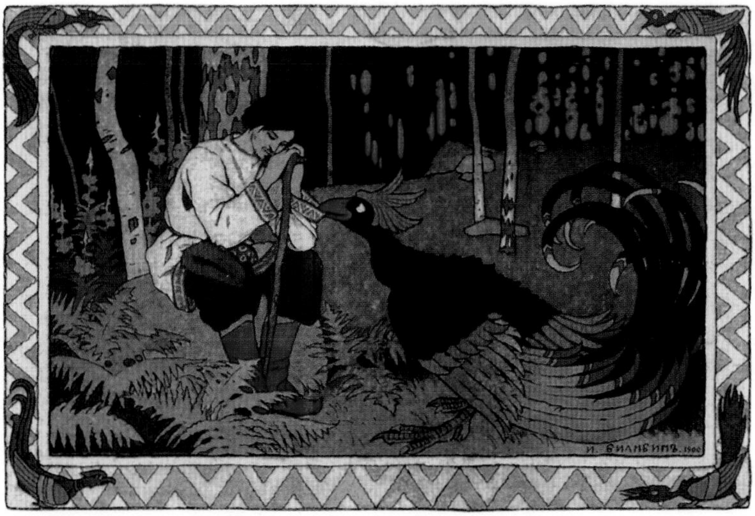

Ivan the Fool and his valuable friend

Glossary

beacon A guiding signal or symbol, usually high up.

bridle Headgear for a horse, used to control and lead it.

emerge To come up or out of.

gilded Made from or covered with gold.

immortal Not able to die, everlasting.

inscriptions Writings carved into a hard surface.

mane The hair on the back of a horse's neck.

misfortune An unfortunate event or bad luck.

outraged Very angry, offended, or shocked.

quest A mission or search to find something.

shadowed Followed closely behind, like a shadow.

shape-shift To change physical appearance, usually in order to trick someone.

stables Buildings where horses and other animals are kept.

undertake To begin a task or an attempt.

INDEX